Pussy cat, pussy cat, where have you been?

I've been to **Rome**,
and guess what I've seen…

Russell Punter

Illu̶st̶ra̶te̶d̶ ̶by̶ ̶Gi̶an̶a̶ ̶T̶ay̶lor

Pussy cat, pussy cat,
where have you been?

I've been to Rome,
and guess what I've seen...

People called Romans built Rome long ago.
You'll see their old buildings wherever you go.

Gladiators fought in the huge Colosseum.
Hundreds of Romans came here just to see them.

Sometimes wild animals filled the arena.
There were panthers and lions, wild boar and hyena.

At the Circus Maximus chariot races,
riders and horses were put through their paces.

The charioteers whizzed around and around.
When the racing was over, the winner was crowned.

The rulers of Rome came to meet at the Forum.
You can still see the ruins – I went to explore them.

Speeches were made here when battles were won.
And at Trajan's Market, big business was done.

Il Vittoriano was built for a king.
The Kingdom of Italy started with him.

King Victor
Emmanuel II

The Quirinale Palace is the President's home.
It has grand rooms to visit and gardens to roam.

At the fine Trevi Fountain, so some people say,
if you toss in a coin, then you'll come back one day.

Climb the steep Spanish Steps and they'll take you up high.
They're named after an embassy once found nearby.

The Pantheon Temple is a highlight of Rome.
Bright sunshine pours in through a hole in the dome.

The Piazza Navona has cafés to try.
The Fountain of Four Rivers trickles nearby.

Castel Sant'Angelo was used during wars.
Popes had their apartments behind its strong doors.

The Vatican Museums hold great works of art.
The hushed Sistine Chapel is the most famous part.

There are scenes from the Bible all over the ceiling.
With so much to look at, it left my head reeling.

Saint Peter's Basilica stands in a square.
I followed the crowds who were gathering there.

They looked up at Saint Peter's, and waited in hope.
Their wish was soon granted, when out came the Pope!

You packed in a lot there,
before you came home.

I had such a good time.
There's no place like Rome!

Edited by Jane Chisholm

First published in 2018 by Usborne Publishing Ltd., Usborne House, 83-85 Saffron Hill,
London EC1N 8RT, England. www.usborne.com Copyright © 2018 Usborne Publishing Ltd.

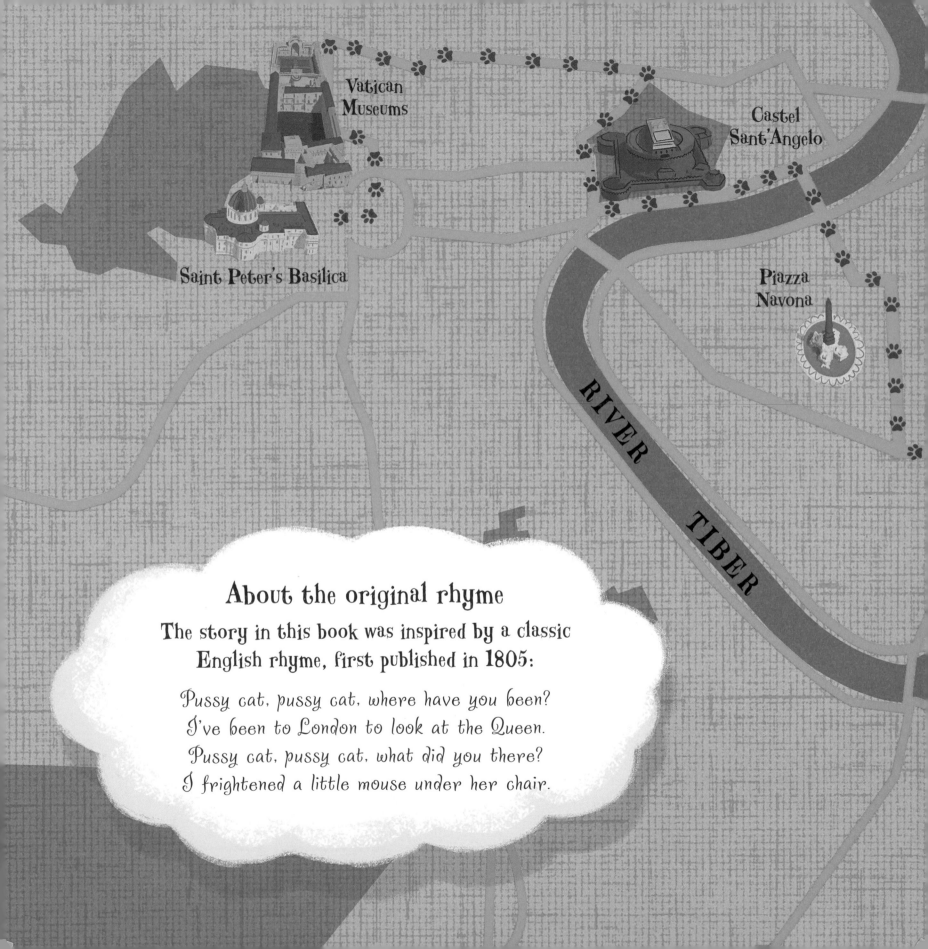

Vatican
Museums

Castel
Sant'Angelo

Saint Peter's Basilica

Piazza
Navona

RIVER TIBER

About the original rhyme

The story in this book was inspired by a classic
English rhyme, first published in 1805:

Pussy cat, pussy cat, where have you been?
I've been to London to look at the Queen.
Pussy cat, pussy cat, what did you there?
I frightened a little mouse under her chair.